DARE TO RUN

to Don Barkhouse
from John Shaerer
11/4/90 Heb. 2:12

SONGBOOK

51 CONTEMPORARY SONGS

COMPILED BY KEN BIBLE

ADVISORY COMMITTEE

TOM FETTKE
LYNDELL LEATHERMAN
ALAN JOHNSON

Lillenas PUBLISHING COMPANY
KANSAS CITY, MO 64141

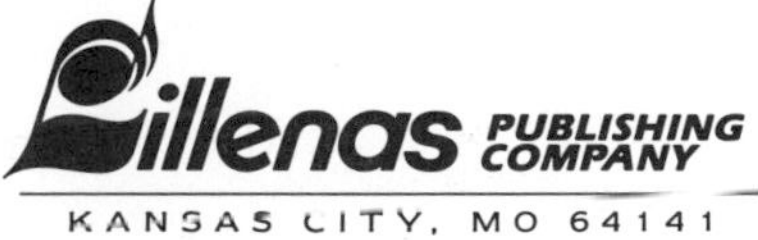

Yes, Lord, Yes

1
L. K.
LYNN KEESECKER
♩ = ca. 116
Yes, Lord, yes! to Your will and to Your way.
Yes, Lord, yes! I will trust You and o - bey.
When Your Spir - it speaks to me, with my whole heart I'll a - gree.
And my an - swer will be yes, Lord, yes, Lord, yes!
yes!

Awesome God

2
R. M.
RICH MULLINS
♩ = 72
Our God is an awe-some God; He reigns from heav-en a-bove with wis-dom, pow'r, and love. Our God is an awe-some God! Our God! Our God is an awe-some God! Our God is an awe-some God! Our God is an awe-some God!

© 1988 Edward Grant, Inc.

Shine Down

B. S., M. G., and B. F.

BILLY SMILEY, MARK GERSMEHL and BOB FARRELL

Shine down Your light on me; Let the peo - ple see
that in Your pres - ence dark - ness flees.
Fa -ther of light, shine down on me.
Fa - ther of light, shine down on me.
*1. There's a land full of glo - ry
2. There's no sun in that cit - y,
in a place where there is
the Fa-ther's throne is its on-

*Verse 1 on recording.

no night;___ And in that ho - ly cit - y
- ly light;___ ______ The lamp of sal - va - tion,
burns the bea - con of ev - er - last - ing light;___
the hope that is al - ways glow - ing bright.___
The light that keeps reach - ing to the peo-ple of ev -
It scat-ters the dark - ness, swept a-way by His might-
- 'ry land,___ ______ A love that is long - ing
- y hand;___ Now all the na - tions can wor - ship,
to fill the heart__ of ev - 'ry__ man.___
sing the song of that glo - rious Lamb.

4 **F**riends

M. W. S. and D. D. S.
MICHAEL W. SMITH and DEBORAH D. SMITH
Unison
1. Pack-ing up__ the dreams__ God plant-ed
2. With the faith_ and love___ God's giv-en,
In the fer - tile soil__
Spring-ing from the hope
___ of you;__
___ we know,__
Can't be-lieve__ the hopes__ He's
We will pray__ the joy___ you'll
grant-ed
live in
Means a chap-ter in__ your life__ is through.__
___ Is the strength that now__ you show.__
But we'll keep you close___ as al - ways;
It won't e -
- ven seem__ you've gone,___ 'Cause our__ hearts in big and

small ways Will keep the love that keeps us strong.
And friends are friends for-ev - er If the Lord's the Lord of them.
And a friend will not say "nev-er" 'Cause the wel-come will not end. Though it's
hard to let you go, In the Fa-ther's hands we know That a
life - time's not too long to live as friends.

Always There for You

M. S., R. S., O. F., T. G.

MICHAEL SWEET, ROBERT SWEET,
OZ FOX, and TIMOTHY GAINES

♩ = ca. 58
I'm al - ways there for you. I'll
al - ways stand by you. When the world
has closed the door, and you can't go on
an - y-more, I'm al - ways there for you.
I'm there for you.

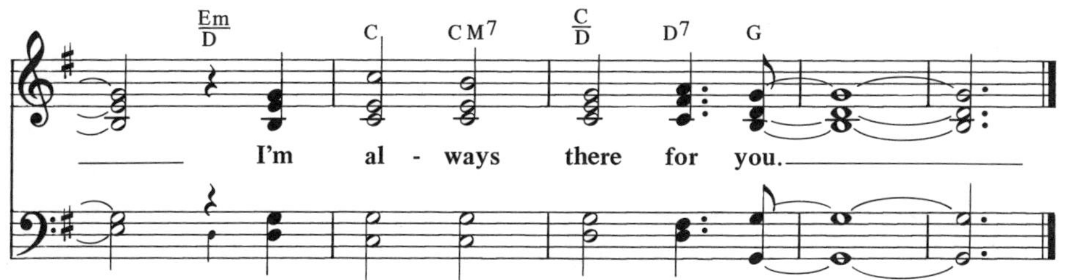

Em/D   C   CM7   C/D   D7   G
I'm al - ways there for you.

6 **B**e Still and Know

Adapted

Unknown
Arr. by Tom Fettke

G   C   F   C/E   G7/D   C   G   G7/B   C
1. Be____ still____ and know____ that I____ am God. Be
2. I____ am____ the Lord____ that heal - eth thee. I
3. In____ Thee,____ O Lord,____ I put____ my trust. In

G7/D   C/E   F   F/Eb   D   Em7   D7/F#   G   G/F
still____ and know that I____ am God. Be
am____ the Lord that heal - eth thee. I
Thee,____ O Lord, I put____ my trust. In

C/E   C   Dm7   C/E   C   F   C/G   G7   C
still____ and know____ that I____ am God.
am____ the Lord____ that heal - eth thee.
Thee,____ O Lord____ I put____ my trust.

He is Exalted

T. P.

TWILA PARIS

♩. = ca. 66
He is ex-alt-ed, the King is ex-alt-ed on high; I will
praise Him. He is ex-alt-ed, for-ev-er ex-alt-ed, and
I will praise His name! He is the
Lord; for-ev-er His truth shall reign. Heav-en and
earth re-joice in His ho-ly name. He is ex-alt-ed, the

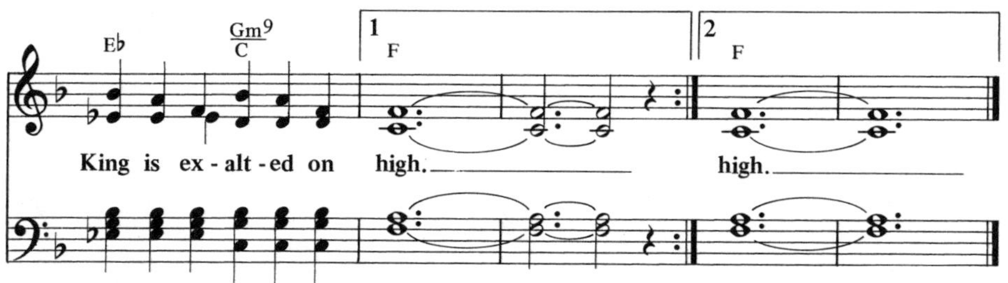

Eb   Gm9/C   1 F   2 F
King is ex-alt-ed on high._______ high._______

8. I Love You, Lord

L. K.

LAURIE KLEIN
Arr. by Eugene Thomas

♩ = ca. 84   Eb   Bb   Eb
I love You, Lord,______ and I lift my voice______ to
Ab Eb/Bb Bb7 Eb/Bb Bb Bbsus Bb Eb
wor-ship You. O my soul, re-joice! Take joy, my King,______
Bb Eb Eb7
______ in______ what You hear:______ may it be a
Ab Eb/Bb Bb Bb7 Eb Ab/Eb Eb
sweet, sweet______ sound in______ Your ear.______

Shut De Do

R. S.

RANDY STONEHILL

Latin feel ♩ = ca. 84
G
Am G
Am
Shut de dō, keep out de dev-il. Shut de dō, keep de dev-il in de
de dō
de dev-il
Bm G
Am G
C
G/B
night. Shut de dō, keep out de dev-il. Light de can - dle, ev-'ry-
de dō
de dev-il
Am
Last time to Coda
G
C
G/B
Am7 D7 G
Solo optional
thin's al - right. Light de can - dle, ev - 'ry - thin's al-right. 2. My
*1. Oh,
*3. Oh,
G
Group
when I was a ba - by child,
ma - ma used to sing this song, Shut de dō, keep
sa - tan is an e - vil charm - er;

*Verses 1 and 3 on recording.

Am/E G/D Solo G Group
Good and bad was just a game.
— out de dev-il; Pa-pa used to sing it, too. Shut de dō,
He's hun-gry for a soul to hurt.
Am Bm Solo G
— keep de dev-il in de night.
Man-y years and man-y tri-als,
Je-sus called and took them home,
And with-out your ho-ly ar-mor,
Group Am/E G/D Solo G
They proved to me they're not the same.
Shut de dō, keep out de dev-il; And so I sing this song for you.
He will eat you for des-sert.
Group G Am Bm D.C. CODA C G/B
Shut de dō, keep de dev-il in de night. Light de can-dle, ev-'ry-
Am G C G/B Am7 D7 G rit.
thin's al-right. Light de can-dle, ev-'ry-thin's al-right.

10. Great Are You Lord

S. C. and V. C.
STEVE and VIKKI COOK
♩ = ca. 96

Ho - ly Lord, most ho - ly Lord, You a - lone are wor - thy
of my praise._ O ho - ly Lord, most ho - ly Lord, with
all of my heart I sing._ Great are You,
Lord; wor - thy of praise,_ ho -
ly and true. Great are You, Lord, most ho - ly Lord._

Destined to Win

E. D. and D. K.

EDDIE DeGARMO and DANA KEY

Unison
We are___ des - tined to win;___ We're sur-round-
-ed by His love, guard - ed by His pow - er.___ Des-tined to win;___
___ fol - low-ing the Lord un-til___ the bat-tle's o - ver.___
We are___ des - tined___ to___ win.___
We are___ win.___

Blessed Be the Lord God Almighty

BOB FITTS

B. F.
Unison
Fa-ther in heav-en, how we love You; We lift Your name in
all the earth. May Your king-dom be es-tab-lished in our
prais - es, As Your peo-ple de-clare Your might-y works. Bless-ed be the
Lord God al - might - y, Who was, and is and is to
come. Bless-ed be the Lord God al - might - y, Who

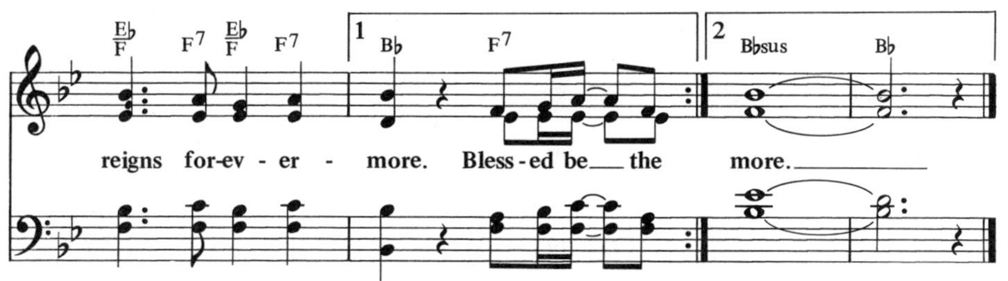
reigns for-ev - er - more. Bless-ed be the more.

13 Cares Chorus

KELLY WILLARD

I cast all my cares up-on You. I
lay all of my bur-dens down at Your feet; And
an-y-time that I don't know what to do, I will
cast all my cares up-on You.

14   *How Excellent is Thy Name*

D. T., M. T. and P. S.
DICK TUNNEY, MELODIE TUNNEY and PAUL SMITH
= ca. 152
How ex-cel-lent is Thy name, O Lord, How
ex-cel-lent is Thy name! Heav-en and earth to-
geth-er pro-claim how ex-cel-lent is Thy name! How
ex-cel-lent is Thy name!
Solo or unison
1. I look in-to
2. One fine day
Last time:
Fine
the mid-night blue and see the work You've done..
when the trum-pets play and the dead in Christ shall rise,

Your chil - dren raise a per - fect praise
The cho - sen few will gath - er to
while en - e - mies hold their tongue. Cre -
pro - claim You Lord Most High. With
a - tion shows Your splen - dor, Your reign - ing maj - es -
joy - ful al - le - lu - ias the heav - en - ly host will
ty, And yet I find You take the time
sing. Ev - 'ry knee shall bow and tongue will shout,
to care for one like me! How
"You are the King of Kings."
D.S. (twice)

We Are an Offering

15
We Are an Offering
D. L.
DWIGHT LILES
♩ = ca. 60
We lift our voic - es,— we lift our hands,— we lift our lives— up to
voic - es; Lord, use our hands; Lord, use our lives, they are
You; We are an of-fer-ing.—— Lord, use our
Yours; We are an of -fer-ing.——
All that we have,—— all that we are,—— All that we
hope to be we give to You, we give to You.——
We lift our voic - es,—— we lift our hands,—— we lift our

lives up to You; We are an of-fer-ing, we are an of-fer-ing.

16   *What a Mighty God We Serve*

Author Unknown

Composer Unknown
Arr. by Keith Phillips

What a might-y God we serve.
What a might-y God we serve.
An-gels bow be-fore Him, heav-en and earth a-dore Him;
What a might-y God we serve.

First Love

BOB HARTMAN

JOHN ELEFANTE

Cut time feel ♩ = 104
First Love, First Love, my soul longs af - ter You.
First Love, my First Love, I want my
heart to stay so true. Be - cause You first loved me,
Je - sus, You will al - ways be,
You will al - ways be my First Love.

I Love You with the Love of the Lord

JAMES GILBERT

J. G.

I love you with the love of the Lord,
Yes, I love you with the love
of the Lord. I can see in
you the glo - ry of my King, And I
love you with the love of the Lord.

I, the Lord, Will Answer

19
I, the Lord, Will Answer
D. W.
Based on Isaiah 41:17-20
(*2-part Round)
DAN WHITTEMORE
Arr. by Tom Fettke
I Unison
Dm
A7 Dm
The__ poor and need-y search for wa-ter; Their tongues are parched with
A7 Dm
thirst, but wa-ter can-not be found. Oh,__ who will they turn to;
A7 Dm
Dm A7 Dm II
Where will they go? Oh,__ what can sat-is-fy them in a dry, bar-ren land?
Dm
A7 Dm
I, the Lord,__will an-swer; hear Me well. I will not__ for-sake you, O__
A7 Dm
Dm
A7 Dm
Is-ra-el. I, the Lord,__will an-swer; hear Me well.

*Sing the complete song in unison. Then, on the repeat, sing as a round.

I will not for-sake you, O Is - ra - el. Is - ra - el.

20

Honor Him

D. K. and N. B.

DON KOCH and NILES BOROP

Hon - or Him to whom hon - or is due. Glo - ri - fy Him
whose glo - ry shines through. Lift up the Lord our
God, for He has made all things new!
Hon - or Him to whom hon - or is due.

I Believe in You

M. S., R. S., O. F., T. G.
MICHAEL SWEET, ROBERT SWEET, OZ FOX, and TIMOTHY GAINES
= ca. 84
Unison
I be - lieve in You, O
through and through; Al - ways
and for - ev - er it will be
You and me to - geth - er. I be -

2
Dbadd9   Db   Cm   Bb   Ab/Bb   Bb   Ebsus   Eb
be You___ and me.   I will   sing   to You___
Bb/D   C sus   Cm   Cm/Bb
___   and all You do.___
Abadd9   Ab   Ebsus   Eb
Al - ways___ and for - ev - er it will
Dbadd9   Dbadd9/C   Bb7
be   You and me___   to -
Cm   Cm/Bb   Ab   Bb   C
geth - er.___   Oo___

Glorify Thy Name

DONNA ADKINS

D. A.

♩ = ca. 100

*1. Fa - ther, we love You, we wor - ship and a -
*2. Je - sus, we love You, we wor - ship and a -
3. Spir - it, we love You, we wor - ship and a -
dore You;
dore You; Glo - ri - fy Thy name in all the earth.
dore You;
Glo - ri - fy Thy name, glo - ri - fy Thy name,
Glo - ri - fy Thy name in all the earth.

*Verses 1 and 2 on recording.

Great Is the Lord

M. W. S. and D. D. S.

MICHAEL W. SMITH and DEBORAH D. SMITH

Great is the Lord, He is ho - ly and just; By His
pow - er we trust in His love.
Great is the Lord, He is faith - ful and
true; By His mer - cy He proves He is love.

1. 2. Great is the Lord and wor - thy of glo - ry!
(D.S.)3. Great are You, Lord, and wor - thy of glo - ry!
Great is the Lord and wor - thy of praise.
Great are You, Lord, and wor - thy of praise.
Great is the Lord; now lift up your voice, Now
Great are You, Lord; I lift up my voice, I
lift up your voice: Great is the
lift up my voice: Great are You,
Lord! Great
Lord! Great

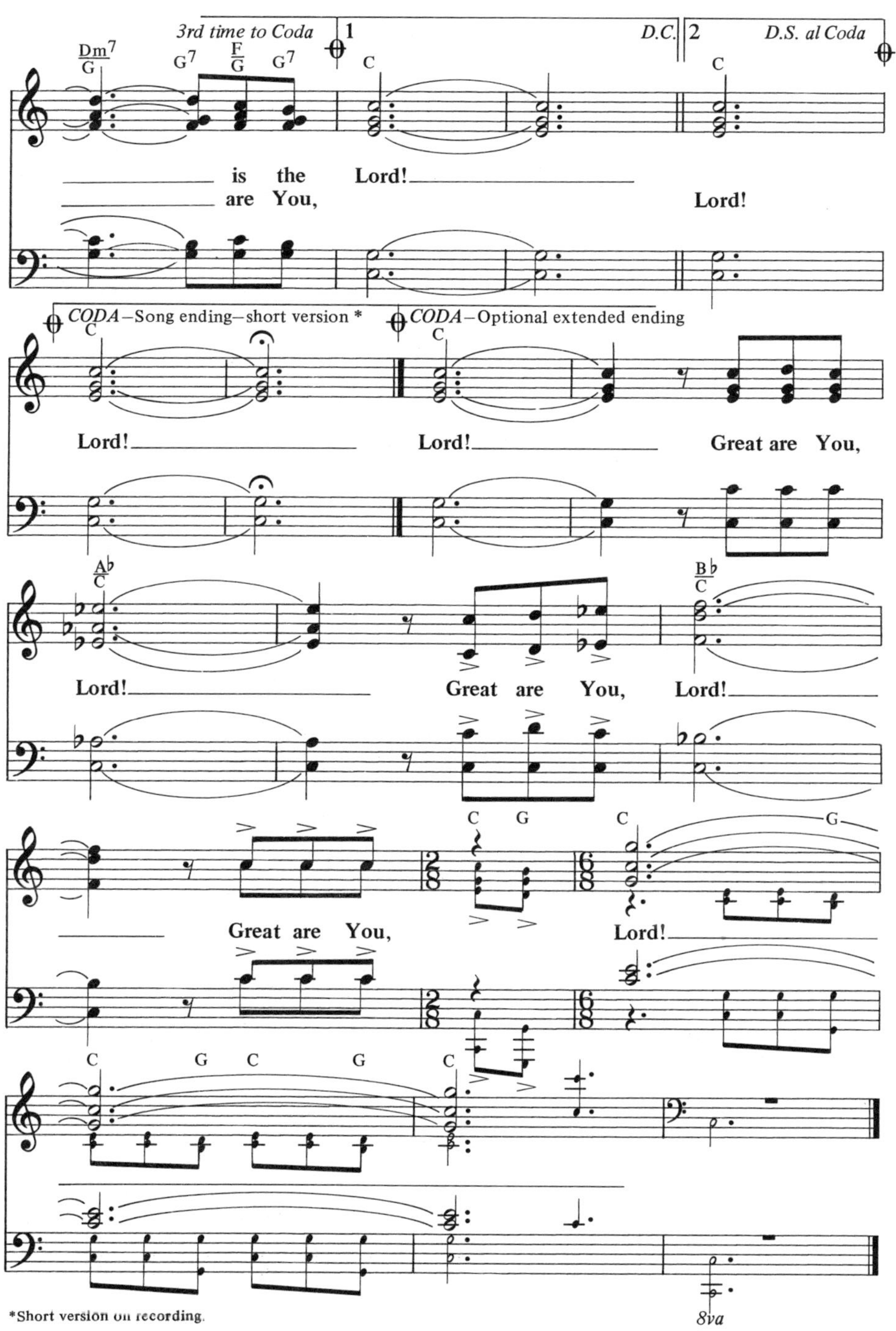

3rd time to Coda
1
D.C.
2
D.S. al Coda
Dm7/G
G7
F/G
G7
C
C
is the Lord!
are You, Lord!
CODA—Song ending—short version *
CODA—Optional extended ending
C
C
Lord!
Lord!
Great are You,
Ab/C
Bb/C
Lord!
Great are You, Lord!
C
G
C
G
Great are You,
Lord!
C
G
C
G
C
*Short version on recording.
8va

Make Me a Servant

K. W.
KELLY WILLARD
= 92
Make me a ser - vant, hum - ble and meek.
Lord, let me lift up those who are weak.
And may the prayer of my heart al - ways be:
Make me a ser - vant, make me a ser - vant,
Make me a ser - vant to - day, to - day.
to - day.

Find Us Faithful

J. M.
JON MOHR
= ca. 69
Oh, may all who come be-hind us find us faith - ful,
May the fire of our de-vo - tion light their way. May the
foot - prints that we leave Lead them to be - lieve, And the
lives we live in-spire them to o - bey. Oh, may
all who come be - hind us find us faith - ful.

O Magnify the Lord

M. T. and D. T.
MELODIE and DICK TUNNEY
♩ = ca. 100
1. O mag-ni-fy,— O mag-ni-fy— the Lord—with me, And
(2. O) wor-ship Him,— O wor-ship Christ— the Lord—with me, And
let us ex-alt His name to-geth-er! O
let us ex-alt His name to-geth-er! O
mag-ni-fy— the Lord, O mag-ni-fy— the Lord, And may His
wor-ship Christ,—the Lord; O wor-ship Christ,—the Lord; And may His
Last time to Coda
name be lift-ed—high for-ev-er! 2. O er!
King of— Kings and Lord—of— Lords,— May His name be

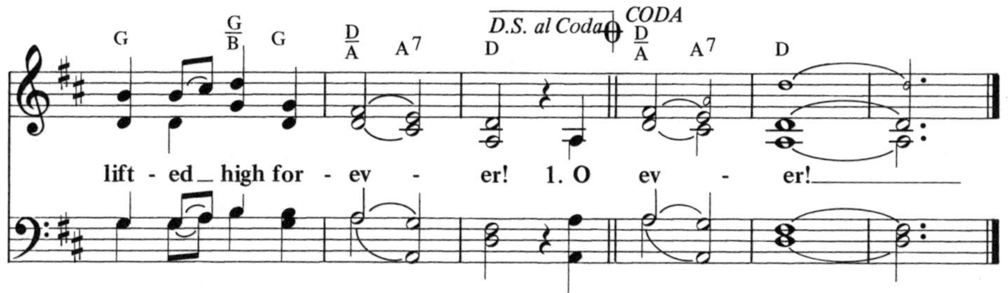

D.S. al Coda
CODA
lift - ed _ high for - ev - er! 1. O ev - er!

27 Open Our Eyes

BOB CULL

B. C.

♩ = ca. 108

1. O - pen our eyes, Lord, _____ we want to see Je - sus; _____
2. O - pen our ears, Lord, _____ and help us to lis - ten; _____
_____ To reach out and _ touch Him, _____ and say that we love
_____ ♪ O - pen our _ eyes,
Him. _____ Lord, _____ we want to see Je - sus. _____

Let There Be Praise

M. T. and D. T.

MELODIE and DICK TUNNEY

Let there be praise, let there be joy in our
hearts. Sing to the Lord, give Him the glo - ry,
glo - ry glo - ry. Let there be praise, let there be joy in
our hearts. For - ev - er - more let His love
glo - ry

3rd time Fine
Unison
fill the air,— and let there— be praise. 1. He in - hab-its the praise of His
2. When the Spir-it of God is with -
peo-ple, and dwells deep— with - in. The— peace that He gives— none can
in us, we will o - ver - come. In our weak-ness His strength will de-
e - qual; His— love, it knows no end. So lift your
fend us when His praise is on our tongue.
voic - es;— with glad - ness sing. Pro - claim through
all the earth — that Je - sus Christ is King! King!
D.C.
D.C. al Fine

29 Come, Let Us Worship and Bow Down

Psalm 95:6,7; adapted by Dave Doherty
DAVE DOHERTY
Come, let us
wor - ship and __ bow __ down; Let us kneel be-fore the
Lord our God, our Mak - er. Mak - er. For

G   D/F#   Em7   D/F#   G   D/F#   G
He________ is our God, and we are the peo-ple of His
G/A   A   G   A   D   A/C#   Bm   Bm/A
pas - ture; And the sheep________ of His hand, just the
rit. 2nd time only
G   A   G/A   A
1 D   D.S.   2 D
sheep________ of His hand.   hand.

I'm Yours

GARY CHAPMAN

G. C.
♩ = ca. 88
F Bb F Bb
I'm Yours, Lord; ev - 'ry-thing_ I've got, ev - 'ry-thing _ I
F Bb F C7 F
am, ev - 'ry-thing_ I'm not. I'm Yours, Lord;
3rd time to Coda
Bb F Bb F/C C7 C7sus
try me now_ and see, see if I_ can be com-plete -ly
F
Yours.
*1. My life and my love I
2. You put in us all de -

*Verse 1 on recording.

leave in Your hands; I'll glad - ly per - form___ as
sire to be - long, to join with Your strength___ and
Your will de - mands. I know it's not much, Your
thus be - come strong. With that thought in mind, I
gift to re - pay; But it's all I can
reach for the prize; I___ lift up my
give,___ and all I can say is I'm
voice___ to re - em - pha - size that I'm
Yours,
see if I___ can be com - plete - ly Yours. Yours.

31
He Will Carry You
S. W. B.
SCOTT WESLEY BROWN
There is no prob - lem too big— God can-not solve it.
There is no storm too dark— God can-not calm it.
(solve it.)
(calm it.)
There is no moun - tain too tall— He can-not
There is no sor - row too deep— He can-not
1,3
move it.
(move it.)
2,4
soothe it.
If He car-ried the weight of the world up -on His shoul
der, shoul - der, I know, my broth-er, that He will car - ry

you. If He car-ried the weight of the world
shoul - der, up-on His shoul - der, shoul-der, I know, my sis - ter, that
2nd time to Coda
He will car - ry you. He said, "Come un - to
Me all who are wea - ry and I will
give you rest." you.
D.C. al Coda CODA
great rit.
molto rit.

Cornerstone

LEON PATILLO

L. P.
♩ = ca. 126
I lay in Zi - on,____ for a foun - da - tion, a
stone. I lay in Zi-on,____ for a foun - da - tion, a____
stone— A tried____ stone, a pre-cious cor-ner-stone, A sure foun-
da - tion,____ a sure foun - da - tion; A tried____ stone, a
pre-cious cor-ner-stone. He that be- liev -eth shall, _ shall not make haste.

33
Gotta Have a Heart
D. A. and N. A.
♩ = ca. 116
DENNIS and NAN ALLEN
Arr. by Tom Fettke
If you have a heart like Je - sus, you'll see a place to do a__ good
deed. If you have a heart like Je - sus, you will want to sow some kind-
- ness seeds.___ You'll find the down and outs__ and the up___ and a-bouts,
___ and the oth-ers some-where be - tween. Got-ta have a heart like Je -
- sus if you wan-na help the peo - ple,___ peo - ple in need.
Last time to Coda

G/D
Unison
Em7
D/F#
*1. Just___ look-ing at peo - ple, you may___ not see___
2. Just___ may-be you're want-ing a place___ to share,___
G
D/F#
Em7
___ what their smiles are meant___ to hide. They___ may not have the kind of
___ but you don't know where to start. There may be some-one liv-ing
D/F#
G add9
A add9   A
tears___ you see,___ but they might be cry - ing in - side.___
right___ next door;___ you won't have to look___ ver - y far.___
G6/A
A/G
F#m7
Bm
Bm/A
Look with your heart___ in-stead___ of your eyes___ to
G
D/F#
Em7
find God's work___ in them. ___________ If you want to be___ like

*Verse 1 on recording.

Je - sus, __ you've got-ta have a heart __ like Him. __
D/F#   G add9   A add9   A
Parts optional
D.S. twice
D   D/F#   CODA   D
If you have a

34   Lord, Be Glorified
B. K.   BOB KILPATRICK
C   G/B   Am   Em7   Dm7
In my life, Lord, be glor-i-
Your church,
Dm7/C   Bb   G7sus   G7   C   G/B
fied, __ be glor-i-fied. __ In my
Your
Am   Em   Dm7   G7sus   G7   F/G   C
life, Lord, be glor-i-fied __ to - day.
church,

Prince of Peace

T. P.

TWILA PARIS

Prince of Peace, come and reign.
Set Your feet on the moun-tain-top a-gain. Take Your
throne, right-ful Lord. Prince of
Peace, come and reign for-ev-er-more.

In His Time

D. B.
♩ = ca. 96
DIANE BALL

1. In His time (in His time), in His time (in His
2. In Your time (in Your time), in Your time (in Your

time); He makes all things beau - ti - ful in His
time); You make all things beau - ti - ful in Your

time (in His time). Lord, please show me ev - 'ry
time (in Your time). Lord, my life to You I

day As You're teach - ing me Your way, That You
bring; May each song I have to sing Be to

do just what You say in Your time (in Your time).
You a love - ly thing in Your time (in Your time).

Keep in Touch

D. A. and N. A.
Swing style

DENNIS and NAN ALLEN
Arr. by D. A. and Tom Fettke

finger snaps
N.C.
1. Let__ your fin-gers do the walk-
2. You__ can al-ways take Him with
- in'__ through the pag-es of God's Word.__ Let__ His Spir-it do the talk-
__you__ an-y-where that you may go,____ If__you keep a good con-nec-
- in'____ to your heart.____ Keep__ in mind a prayer to Him
- tion____ all the time.____ Tune your ear and real-ly lis-
____ all __ through the day and through the night;__ Keep__ in touch
- ten_ 'cause He speaks so loud and clear;____ Keep__ in touch
Gm9

wher - ev-er you are.
wher - ev-er you are.
Don't be a stran - ger,
but keep in touch.
Don't be a stran - ger;
He wants to talk with you so much. Don't be a stran - ger,
but keep in touch;
Al-ways keep in
touch with the Lord.
finger snaps

Give Thanks

H. S.
♩ = ca. 92
HENRY SMITH
Give thanks with a grate-ful heart,__ Give thanks to the
Ho - ly One;__ Give thanks__ be-cause He's giv-en Je - sus
Christ,________ His Son.____ Give Son.____ And
now let the weak say, "I am strong," Let the

poor say, "I am rich," Be-cause of what the
Lord has done for us. And now let the
weak say, "I am strong," Let the poor say, "I am
rich," Be-cause of what the Lord has done for
us. Give us. Give thanks!

Thy Word

MICHAEL W. SMITH

AMY GRANT
Arr. by Keith Phillips

♩ = ca. 76
Unison
Thy Word is a lamp un-to my feet— and a light un-to my
path.
path.
Thy Word is a lamp un-to my feet— and a light un-to my
path.
path.
Thy Word is a

C
F
Gm7
C7
F
Bb/F
F
2nd time Fine
lamp un-to my feet___ and a light un-to my path.

40 — This Is My Prayer

D. H.

DOUG HOLCK

C
Unison
F
G7/F
I want to love You, Lord; I want to
C/E
G7/D
C
C/B
Am
Dm
serve You, Lord; I want to please You, Lord;
1
F/G
G
G/F
Cadd9/E
C/E
This is my prayer.
2
F/G
rit.
G7
F/G
C
This is my prayer.

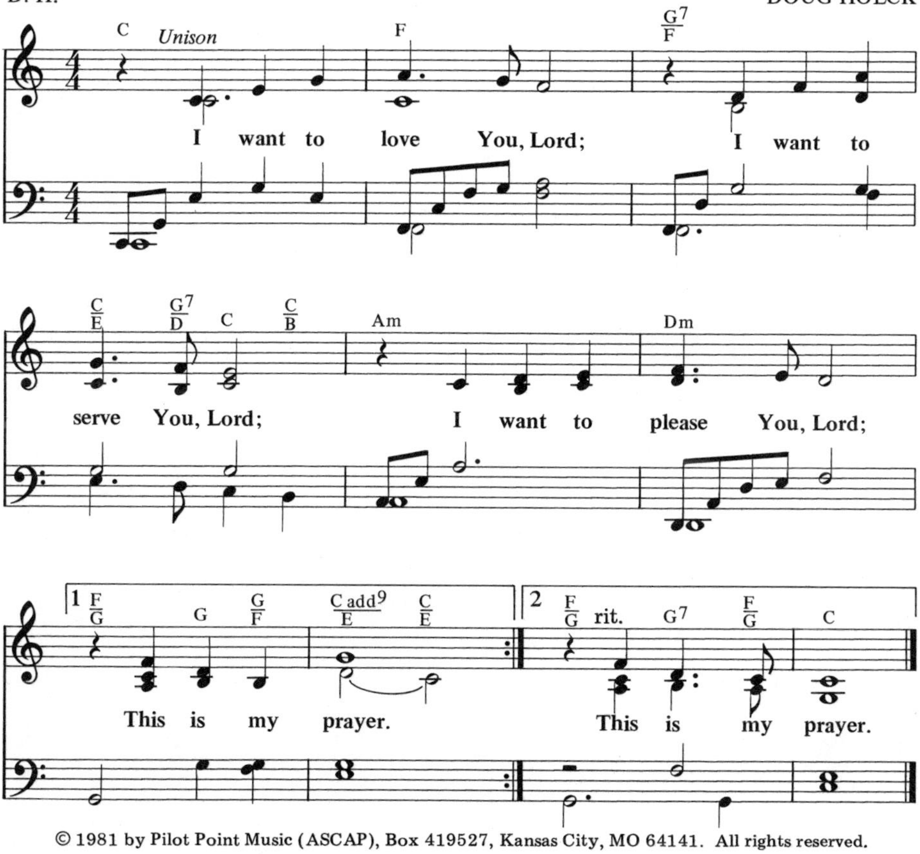

He Who Began a Good Work in You

JON MOHR

J. M.

$\quad$ = ca. 88

Unison
He who be - gan a good work in you,
He who be -
gan a good work in you will be faith-
- ful to com - plete it, He'll be faith-
- ful to com - plete it; He who start -

Am7 G/B C C/D D7 G
- ed the work will be faith - ful to com-plete it in you.

42 King of Kings

(*2-part Round)

SOPHIE CONTY and NAOMI BATYA

Ancient Hebrew Folksong

♩ = 104

Em
I Unison
B7
King of Kings and Lord of Lords, glo - ry, hal -

Em
B7
Em
le - lu - jah! King of Kings and Lord of Lords, glo - ry, hal - le - lu - jah!

II
B7
Em
Je - sus, Prince of Peace, glo - ry, hal - le - lu - jah! Je - sus,

B7
Em
N.C.
Prince of Peace, glo - ry, hal - le - lu - jah!

*Sing the song through once in unison. Then, on the repeat, sing as a round.

Called to Holiness

D. L. and N. B.
♩ = ca. 69
DWIGHT LILES and NILES BOROP
We are called to ho-li-ness, Called to re-flect
His righ-teous-ness. No great-er aim could we
ev-er at-tain than this. We are called to
ho-li-ness, To live a life that
He will bless; Yield-ing our way to His will ev-'ry-day, be-

Em7 Bm/F♯ G6 D/A   G/A D/A   A sus A   Em7 Bm/F♯ G M7 A7 sus A7 G/A D
com-ing what we __ pro - fess.____ We are called to__ ho - li - ness.

44 Clean Hands, Pure Heart

J. S. and M. G.

JOHN SLICK and MARK GERSMEHL

Shuffle feel ♩ = ca. 100
C   G/B   F/A   C/G   F   C/E G7sus/D C   G sus
Clean   hands,   a   pure   heart   con - se - crat -ed   to   You;____
G   C   G/B   Dm   Am   C/D
____   O - pen,   bro - ken   in__ all   I
D7   G   E/G   Am   Am/G   F   C/G
say__ and__   do.   Oh,   dear__   Lord,________   give me   clean
G/F   C add9/E C/E   G sus/D G/D   Cadd9 C   G sus G F/G   C sus   C
hands,   a pure____ heart____ shin - ing__ for   You.____

I Will Call Upon the Lord

Adapted by M. O'S.

MICHAEL O'SHIELDS

Optional descant
♩ = 122
Unison
I will call up-on___ the Lord
I will call up-on___ the
Lord
who is wor-thy to___ be praised;
who is wor-thy to___ be praised;
So shall I be
So shall I be saved from my en - e-mies.___
saved from my en - e - mies.___

I will call up-on the Lord.
Lord. The
I will call up-on the Lord.
Lord. The
Lord liv-eth, and bless-ed be the Rock; And let the God of my sal-va-tion be ex-
alt - ed. The Lord liv-eth, and bless-ed be the Rock; And let the God of
my sal-va-tion be ex - alt - ed. The ed.

46 *I Exalt Thee*

P. S., Jr.
PETE SANCHEZ, JR.
♩ = ca. 96
I ex - alt Thee, I ex - alt Thee, I ex -
alt Thee, O Lord. I ex - alt Thee,
I ex - alt Thee, I ex - alt Thee, O
Lord. For Thou, O Lord, art high a-bove all the earth;
Thou art ex - alt - ed far a - bove all gods. For Thou, O
2nd time to Coda

2
C7   Bb/C C7   F   C7   F
D.S. al Coda   CODA
bove all___ gods.___   I ex-   Lord.___________

47   The Word
M. C.
MICHAEL CARD
♩ = ca. 58   Ab Eb/G Fm7   Db   Gb/Db Db   Ab   Eb/G

1. The Word is   liv-ing,   the Word is   light;   The Word de-
2. The Word is   wis-dom,   the Word is   true;   The Word takes
3. The Word is   call-ing   time and a-gain;   The Word is

Fm Eb Db   Gb/Db Db   Eb   Ab Eb/G Fm7   Db   Gb/Db Db

lights my soul,   pre-serves my life.   Ho-ly and hid-den,   for-ev-er
all that's old   and makes it new.   When hearts are bro-ken,   it makes them
griev-ing still   for those in sin.   Come now be-liev-ing   This Word is

Ab   Ab/C Db Eb   Fm Eb Db   Gb/Db Db   Ab/Eb Eb   Ab

new;   The per-fect   sac-ri-fice,   Our Lord,   Je-sus   Christ.
whole;   The One who   paid the price,   Our Lord,   Je-sus   Christ.
true.   The cross speaks this ad-vice,   "Trust me," Je-sus   Christ.

That's What Faith Must Be

M. C.
MICHAEL CARD
♩ = ca. 92
F sus   F   Bb/F   C/F   F   F sus   F   Bb/F   C/F   F
Unison   F sus   F   F sus   F   Gm7   C
To hear____ with my heart, to see____ with my soul, to be guid-ed by a hand I can-
F   Dm   Gm7   C   F   C/E   Dm
- not hold;__ To trust____ in a way that I can - not see,___ that's_
Gm7   C7   1,2 C/F Bb/F F   3 F C/F Bb/F F
___ what faith__ must be.________   To hear__ ________

Your Love Compels Me

D. H.

DOUG HOLCK

Your love com - pels me, Lord, to give as
You would give, To speak as You would speak,
to live as You would live. Your love com -
pels me, Lord, to see as You would see, To
serve as You would serve, to be what You would be.

You Are My Hiding Place

MICHAEL LEDNER

M. L.
♩ = ca. 82
You are my hid - ing place, You al - ways
fill my heart with songs of de - liv - er-ance; When-
ev - er I am a - fraid, I will trust in You.
I will trust in You. Let the weak say,
"I am strong in the strength of the Lord!"

Dare to Run

H. M. and J. W. S.
HARLAN MOORE and
JOEL W. SMITH
= 72
Unison
G
Cm6/G
The as - sem - bly of the faith - ful, sur - round-ing, yet un - seen,_
road a - head is nar - row, the way is some-times steep,
G
Em7
1 D7sus/A D7/A G add9/B G/B
Is gath-ered as a wit - ness to the race. And
And on - ly the com-mit - ted claim the
C
G/B
G sus/A G/B
on the track a- wait - ing are the run-ners of to-day;_ The call has come for
C
A7/C#
D sus
D
2 D7sus/A D7 B/D#
each to take his place. The prize. But

Em
Eb+
stand-ing at the fin - ish with arms out-stretched to greet_us, Is the
G/D C G/B Am7 D sus accel.
One who has en-dured the race,_ and paid the fin - al price._
A little faster ♩ = 76
D D7 G D/F# C/E C6/E G/D
parts optional
Dare to run with our eyes fixed on Je - sus,
C G/B Am7 G/B C6 C G/D D7
Fol - low-ing_ the foot-steps of the One who's gone be - fore us.
G D/F# Em Am/E B/D# E9sus Em
Dare to run in the pow-er of His Spir - it,

3rd time to Coda
Called to be vic - tors in a race al - read - y
won; dare to run. run. We must have our Sav-ior's
vi - sion, com - pas - sion for the lost; Cour-age for the
D.S. al Coda
fu - ture, love at an - y cost.
CODA
won; dare to run.

T O P I C A L   I N D E X

ALPHABETICAL INDEX